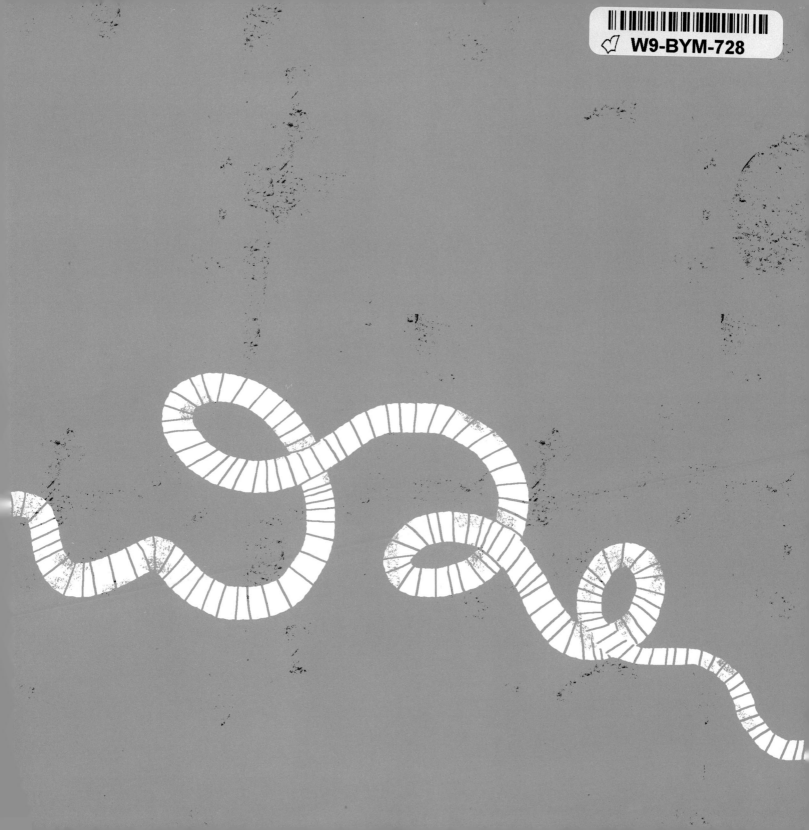

Owlkids Books Inc.
10 Lower Spadina Avenue, Suite 400, Toronto, Ontario M5V 2Z2
www.owlkids.com

North America edition © 2011 Owlkids Books Inc.

Text © 2008 Isabel Minhós Martins
Illustrations © 2009 Yara Kono

Published in Spain under the title *Ovejita, dame lana* © 2010
Kalandraka Ediciones Andalucía
www.kalandraka.com

Distributed in Canada by University of Toronto Press
5201 Dufferin Street, Toronto, Ontario M3H 5T8

Distributed in the United States by Publishers Group West
1700 Fourth Street, Berkeley, California 94710

Library and Archives Canada Cataloguing in Publication

Martins, Isabel Minhós
    Little lamb, have you any wool? / by Isabel Minhós Martins;
illustrated by Yara Kono ; translated by Maureen de Sousa.

Translation of: Ovejita, dame lana.
ISBN 978-1-926973-14-2

    I. Kono, Yara II. De Sousa, Maureen III. Title.

PZ7.M3685Li 2012   j869.3'5   C2011-905822-7

Library of Congress Control Number: 2011935961

Canadian Heritage Patrimoine canadien

Canadä

Ontario
Ontario Media Development Corporation
Société de développement de l'industrie des médias de l'Ontario

Canada Council for the Arts Conseil des Arts du Canada

ONTARIO ARTS COUNCIL
CONSEIL DES ARTS DE L'ONTARIO

We acknowledge the financial support of the Canada Council for the Arts, the Ontario Arts Council, the
Government of Canada through the Canada Book Fund (CBF), and the Government of Ontario through
the Ontario Media Development Corporation's Book Initiative for our publishing activities.

Manufactured by WKT Co. Ltd.
Manufactured in Shenzhen, Guangdong, China, in October 2011
Job #11CB2493

A   B   C   D   E   F

Publisher of Chirp, chickaDEE and OWL
www.owlkids.com

Little Lamb, Have You Any Wool?

Isabel Minhós Martins

Yara Kono

Owl kids

Little lamb, little lamb,
have you any wool?

I want to make a sweater
to keep myself warm.

If I don't cover my belly,
I'll shiver all winter.

Little lamb, little lamb,
have you any more wool?

I'm going to make a handsome
hat to wear upon my head.

Then I won't feel the cold
blowing in my hair or my ears.

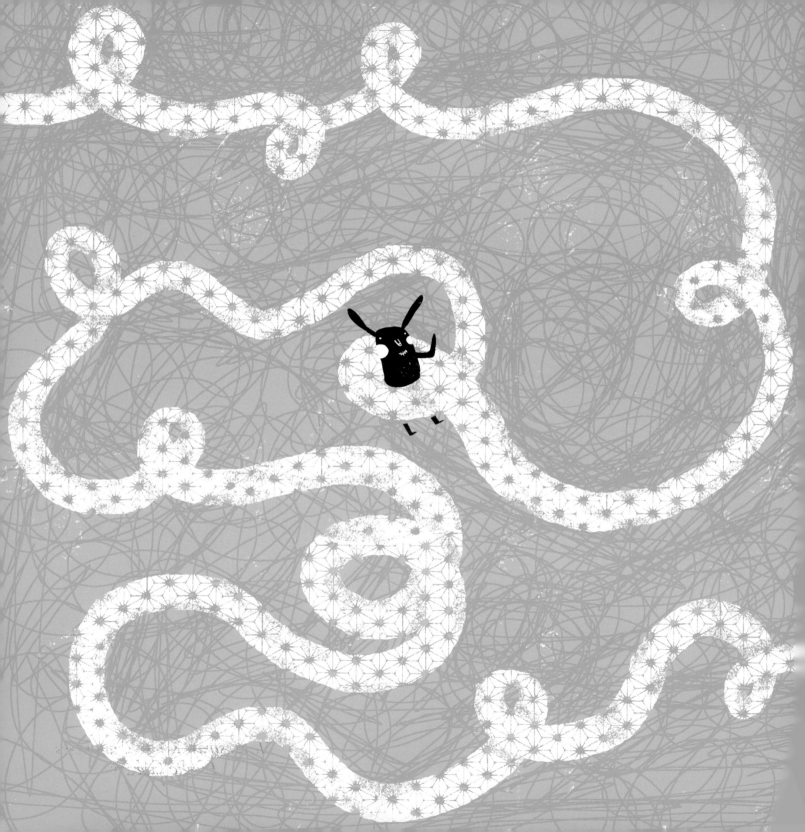

Little lamb, little lamb,
have you even more wool?

I'd like to make a long scarf
to wrap round my neck.

If I don't tie it tight, I'll be
frosty from head to toe.

Little lamb, little lamb,
have you still more wool?

I should make a pair of mittens
to tuck my hands into.

My fingers are as icy as
little icicles.

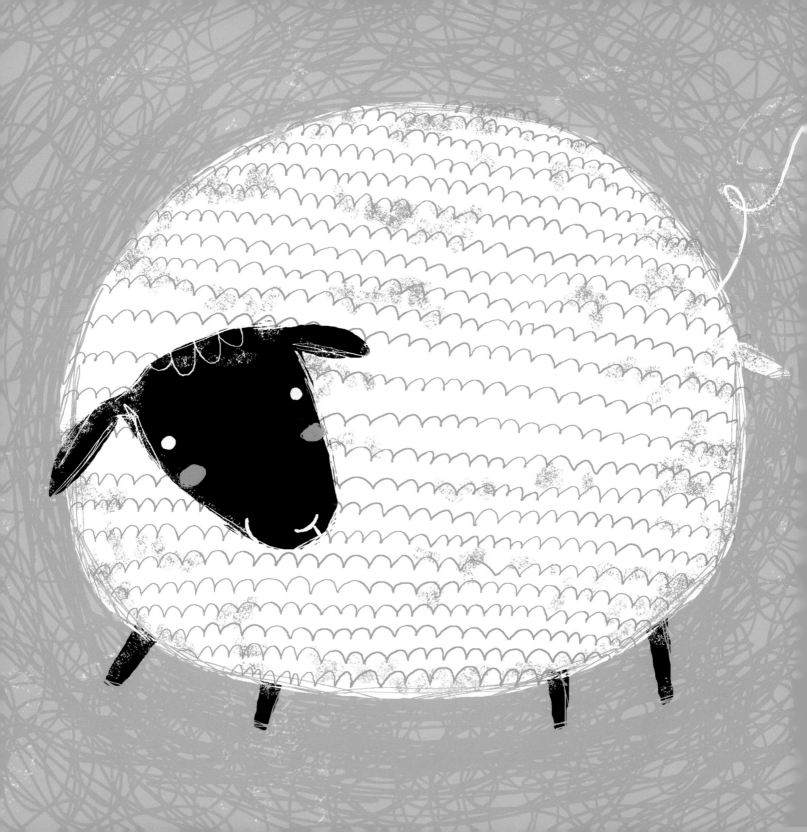

Little lamb, little lamb,
have you a bit more wool?

I want to make a pair of socks
to snuggle over my feet.

My toes are just like little snowballs.

Little lamb, little lamb,
have you just a little bit more wool?

Then I can make a long coat – so
long it will reach the floor!

If I cuddle all up, I won't be afraid
of winter anymore.

Little friend, if you're that cold,
I will let you take my wool and
you can knit it all up.

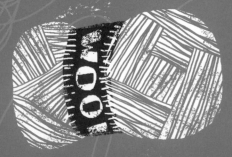

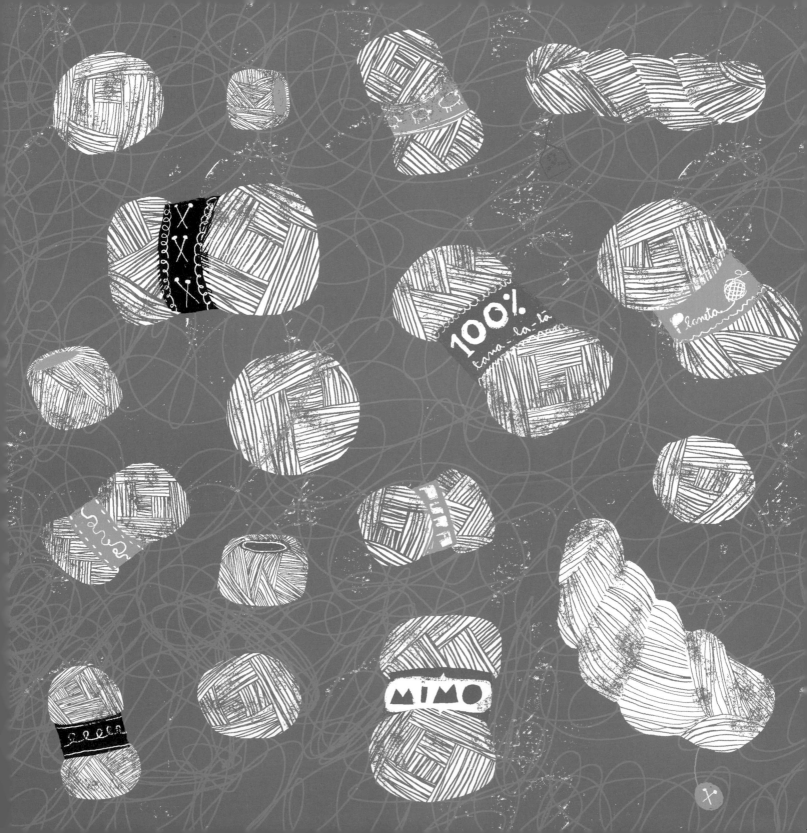

Wool from my belly, wool from my head, wool from my neck, wool from my ears.

Shear it all away, from my head to my toes.

Little lamb, little lamb,
I have used all your wool to
make a scarf, mittens, and socks
to keep myself snug.

And I made another scarf and
other cozy clothes.

Then I realized...I wanted to
share them with you!

So here is a sweater
I have made for you, and
a scarf, and socks, and a hat
to cover your ears.

I made all these clothes with your wool and soft thread.

If they fit you, little lamb, you will say good-bye to the cold.

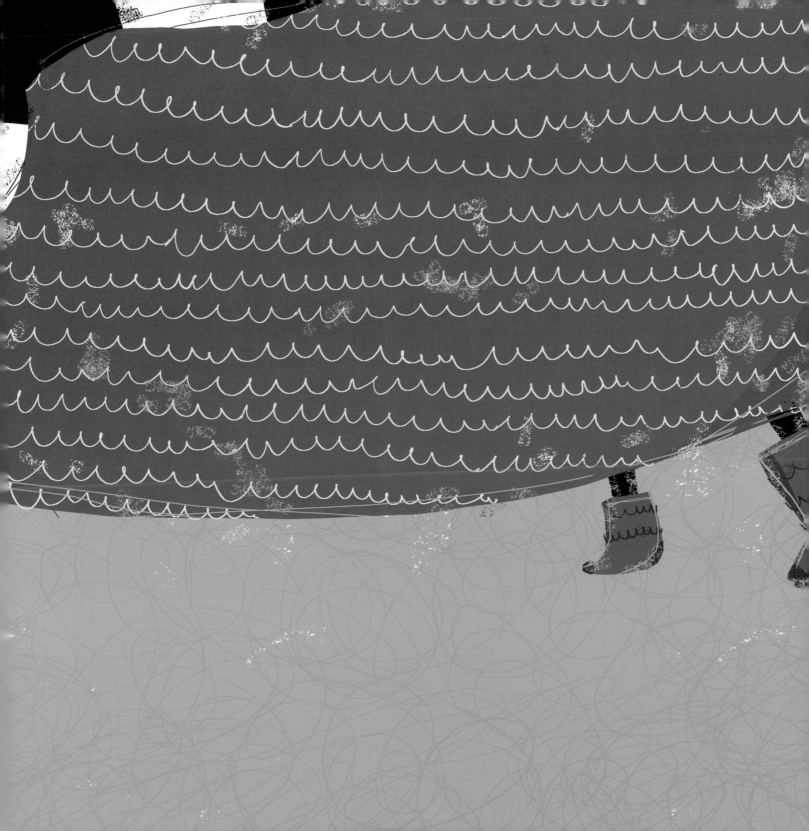

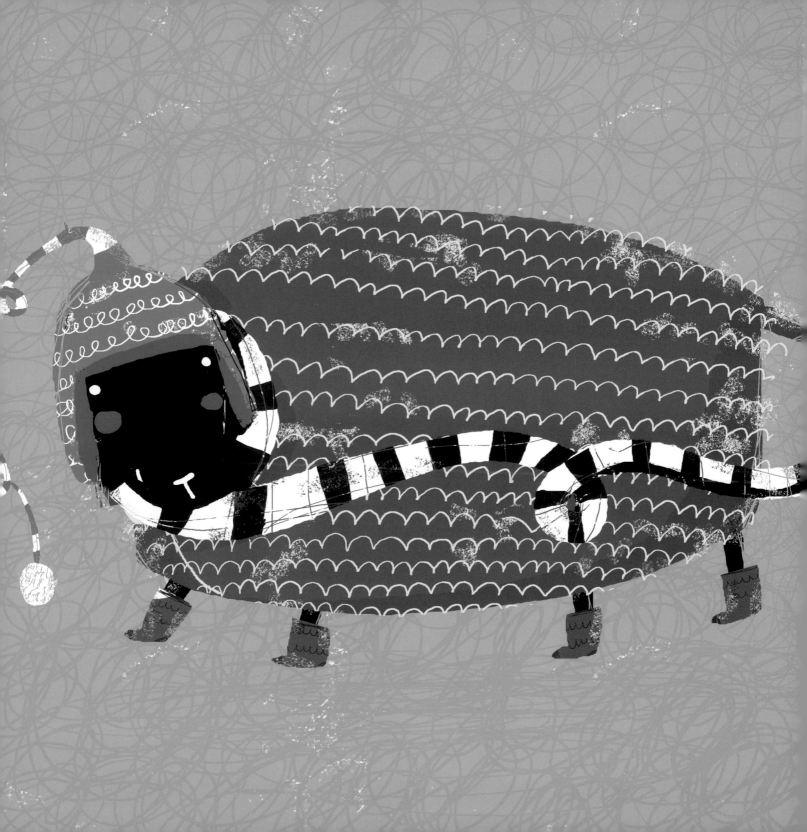

So with these handsome hats
we will cover our heads.

We will enjoy a good winter,
little lamb, you will see!